my itty-bitty bio

Mae Jemison

Cherry Lake Press

Published in the United States of America by Cherry Lake Publishing Group
Ann Arbor, Michigan
www.cherrylakepublishing.com

Reading Adviser: Beth Walker Gambro, MS, Ed., Reading Consultant, Yorkville, IL
Book Designer: Jennifer Wahi
Illustrator: Jeff Bane

Photo Credits: ©Allard One/Shutterstock, 5; © Vadim Sadovski/Shutterstock, 7; © lenetstan/Shutterstock, 9; © 360b/Shutterstock, 11; © Alan C. Heison/Shutterstock, 13; © NASA/ Identifier: ksc-92pc-1881, 15, 22; © Supamotion/Shutterstock, 17; © NASA/Identifier: sts047-37-003, 19, 23; © lev radin/Shutterstock, 21; Cover, 1, 6, 10, 14, Jeff Bane; Various frames throughout, Shutterstock

Cherry Lake Press is an imprint of Cherry Lake Publishing Group.

Library of Congress Cataloging-in-Publication Data

Names: Sarantou, Katlin, author. | Bane, Jeff, 1957- illustrator.
Title: Mae Jemison / by Katlin Sarantou ; illustrated by Jeff Bane.
Description: Ann Arbor, Michigan : Cherry Lake Publishing, [2022] | Series: My itty-bitty bios | Includes index.
Identifiers: LCCN 2021007986 (print) | LCCN 2021007987 (ebook) | ISBN 9781534186859 (hardcover) | ISBN 9781534188259 (paperback) | ISBN 9781534189652 (pdf) | ISBN 9781534191051 (ebook)
Subjects: LCSH: Jemison, Mae, 1956---Juvenile literature. | African American women astronauts--Biography--Juvenile literature. | Astronauts--United States--Biography--Juvenile literature.
Classification: LCC TL789.85.J46 S27 2022 (print) | LCC TL789.85.J46 (ebook) | DDC 629.450092 [B]--dc23
LC record available at https://lccn.loc.gov/2021007986
LC ebook record available at https://lccn.loc.gov/2021007987

Printed in the United States of America
Corporate Graphics

table of contents

About the author: Katlin Sarantou grew up in the cornfields of Ohio. She enjoys reading and dreaming of faraway places.

About the illustrator: Jeff Bane and his two business partners own a studio along the American River in Folsom, California, home of the 1849 Gold Rush. When Jeff's not sketching or illustrating for clients, he's either swimming or kayaking in the river to relax.

my story

My name is Mae Jemison.
I was born in Alabama. It was October 17, 1956. We moved to Illinois.

Welcome to
Sweet Home
Alabama

I love science. One of my favorite TV shows was *Star Trek*. I knew one day I wanted to go to space.

What is your favorite TV show?

I studied hard in college. Then I went on to medical school. I wanted to be a doctor.

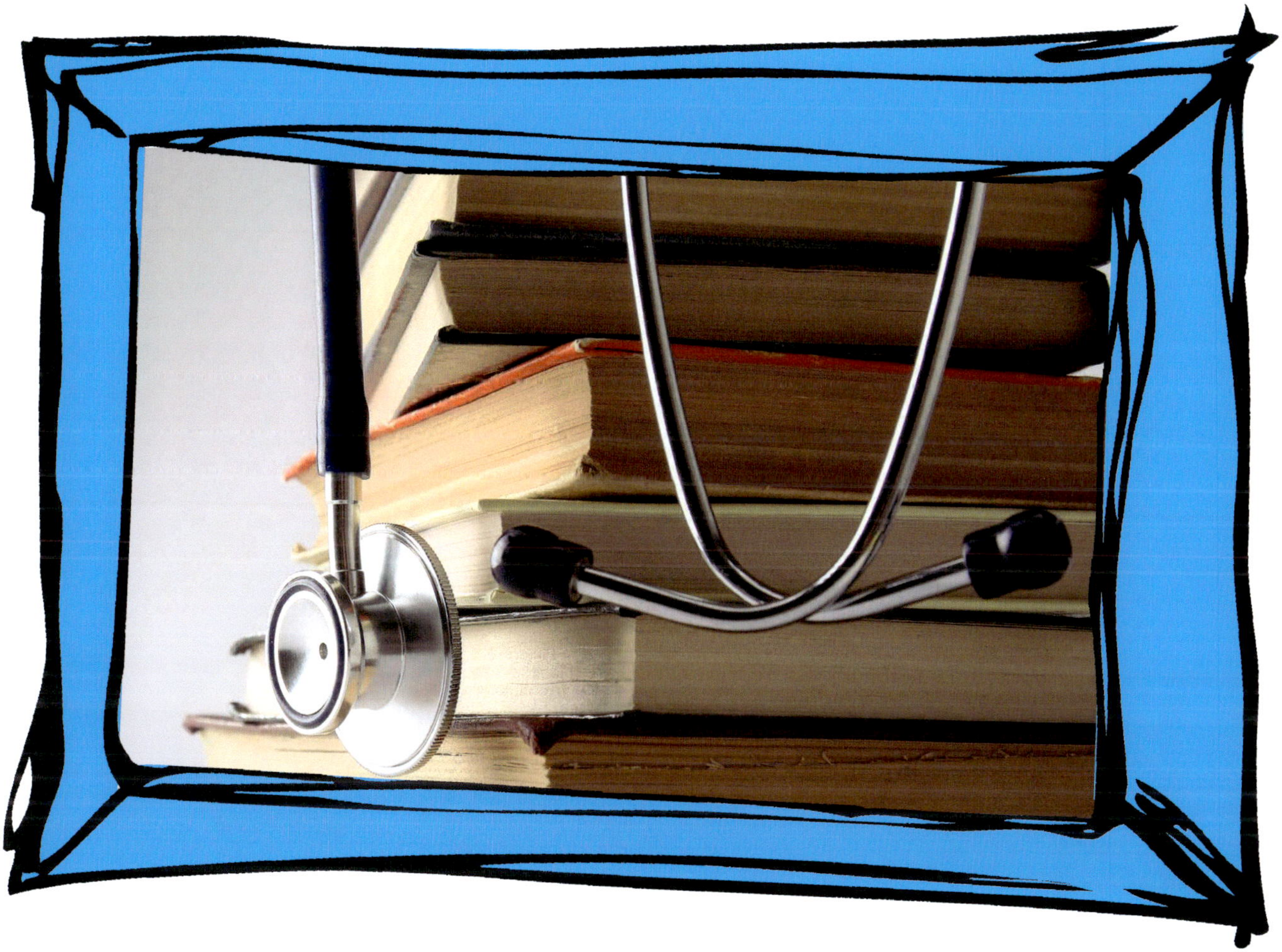

I joined the **Peace Corps** in 1983. I opened my own medical practice.

PEACE CORPS
Peace
Corps

Sally Ride **inspired** me. She was the first American woman in space. I applied to **NASA**. I was accepted in 1987.

Who inspires you?

I was 1 of 15 people chosen. I became the first African American woman to travel to space. This was in 1992.

NASA

I started a company. It supports science and **social** change. I also created an **international** space camp for kids.

I'm in the National Women's Hall of Fame. This happened in 1993. I'm also in the International Space Hall of Fame. This happened in 2004.

I’ve written books and won many awards. I continue to reach for the stars.

What would you like to ask me?

timeline

1992

1950

Born
1956

2004

2060

glossary & index

glossary

college (KOL-ij) a school for higher education

inspired (in-SPYRED) influenced to do something

international (in-tur-NASH-uh-nuhl) open to or involving all nations

NASA (NAH-suh) National Aeronautics and Space Administration

Peace Corps (PEESS KOR) a group of volunteers sent to help underdeveloped nations

social (SOH-shuhl) to do with the way that people live together as a society

index